Malcolm's
Runaway Soap

by Jo Ellen Bogart
illustrated by Linda Hendry

North Winds Press
A Division of Scholastic-TAB Publications Ltd., Richmond Hill, Ontario, Canada

To my husband and best friend, Jim
whose good nature and sense of humour
are such a pleasure

Jo Ellen Bogart

To Mom and Dad
for all the doodle pads

Linda Hendry

Art Director: Kathryn Cole

Text copyright ©1988 by Jo Ellen Bogart. Illustrations copyright ©1988 by Linda Hendry. All rights reserved.

8 7 6 5 4 3 2 1   **Printed in Hong Kong**   89/80123/9

Canadian Cataloguing in Publication Data

Bogart, Jo Ellen, 1945-
  Malcolm's runaway soap

Issued also in French under title: Benoît et le savon volant.
ISBN 0-590-71784-7

I. Hendry, Linda. II. Title.

PS8553.B64M35 1988   jC813'.54   C87-094401-0
PZ7.B64Ma 1988

It all started with Malcolm's bath. Malcolm had been digging
a hole in his backyard and was very dirty. His mother said
he was too dirty to wait for bedtime. He would have to have
a bath in the middle of the afternoon.

"Well," said Malcolm, "if I have to have a bath in the middle of the afternoon, it's going to be a good one." He filled the tub with lots of warm water. Then he played like a seal, splashing and barking and clapping his flippers.

By the time he was ready to start scrubbing, the warm water had made a slippery, squishy mess of his bar of strawberry soap. As Malcolm grabbed it to wash his very dirty knees . . . POP! The soap slipped out of his hands and up into the air.

It landed on the floor, slid along the tiles and raced right out the bathroom door. The soap went past Malcolm's sleeping cat, Ralph, and down the stairs.

When Malcolm's mother opened the front door to get the afternoon paper, the strawberry soap flew between her feet and out onto the front walk.

"Wait!" Malcolm screamed. He ran down the stairs dressed in his favourite blue towel.

"Stop that soap!" he hollered. "Stop that soap!"

The letter carrier saw the speeding soap and ran after it.

"Stop!" she called, but the soap was going faster all the time.

"I've got it!" yelled Policeman Dan, reaching up. He snatched at it with both hands. But . . . POP! The soap flew out of his hands and did a triple back flip. It landed in the paperboy's bag.

"We've got it now!" said the paperboy. He made a grab for the slippery soap. But . . . POP!

The soap sailed right into the jug of lemonade Julie was setting up to sell.

"Malcolm! Is that your soap in my lemonade?" Julie reached in to grab the slimy pink soap, but . . . POP! The soap was off again.

At the end of the block Mr. Sanders was bathing his poodle, Fifi, on the balcony of his apartment. Splash! The flying soap dived right into the bathwater. Fifi nipped at it with her tiny teeth. Mr. Sanders almost got a grip, but ... POP!

The soap landed in Mrs. Abernathy's sun hat.

"Trapped at last!" shouted Malcolm.

Everybody stopped running and started clapping wildly. At last the runaway soap would be caught! But Mrs. Abernathy, who didn't know she had the soap in her hat, thought the applause was for her. She blushed and gave a low bow. Gently, the soap slid down the rim of the hat and fell onto a passing skateboard.

Malcolm saw his strawberry soap zooming off between electric orange running shoes. "Come back!" he shouted to the girl on the skateboard. She screeched to a stop, but the soap kept going.

It flew up and into the window of a bus stopped at the corner. A woman sat on it and ...POP! The soap was off again.

At last it came to rest on a toy sailboat floating in the city hall fountain.

Malcolm saw his chance and leaped into the fountain. He grabbed the soap with both hands and both feet. He washed his ears and his neck, his knees and his ankles, his belly button and his elbows, and even his face. He rubbed until he had a huge, marvellous lather. He scrubbed until the strawberry soap was nothing but bubbles.

When he was squeaky clean, Mrs. Abernathy handed him his favourite blue towel. Malcolm said goodbye to everyone, and Policeman Dan took him home.